The Secret of
SANTA'S ISLAND

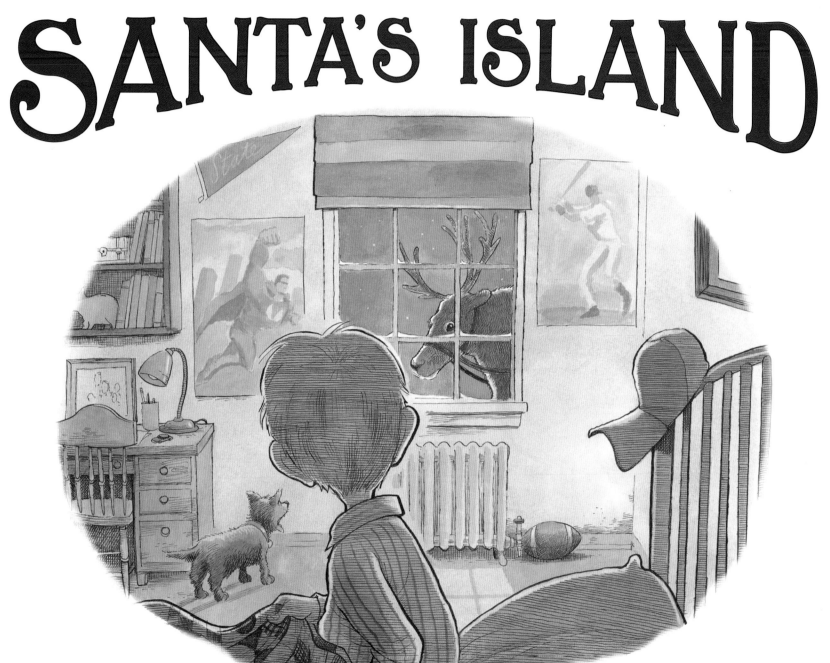

STEVE BREEN

Dial Books for Young Readers
AN IMPRINT OF PENGUIN GROUP (USA) INC.

For Thomas, Patrick, Jack and Jane

DIAL BOOKS FOR YOUNG READERS
A division of Penguin Young Readers Group
Published by The Penguin Group
Penguin Group (USA) Inc., 375 Hudson Street, New York, NY 10014, U.S.A.
Penguin Group (Canada), 90 Eglinton Avenue East, Suite 700, Toronto, Ontario, Canada M4P 2Y3 (a division of Pearson Penguin Canada Inc.)
Penguin Books Ltd, 80 Strand, London WC2R 0RL, England
Penguin Ireland, 25 St. Stephen's Green, Dublin 2, Ireland (a division of Penguin Books Ltd)
Penguin Group (Australia), 250 Camberwell Road, Camberwell, Victoria 3124, Australia (a division of Pearson Australia Group Pty Ltd)
Penguin Books India Pvt Ltd, 11 Community Centre, Panchsheel Park, New Delhi - 110 017, India
Penguin Group (NZ), 67 Apollo Drive, Rosedale, North Shore 0632, New Zealand (a division of Pearson New Zealand Ltd)
Penguin Books (South Africa) (Pty) Ltd, 24 Sturdee Avenue, Rosebank, Johannesburg 2196, South Africa
Penguin Books Ltd, Registered Offices: 80 Strand, London WC2R 0RL, England

Designed by Lily Malcom
Text set in ITC Usherwood
Manufactured in China on acid-free paper

10 9 8 7 6 5 4 3 2 1

Library of Congress Cataloging-in-Publication Data

Breen, Steve.
  The secret of Santa's island / Steve Breen.
      p. cm.
  Summary: Young Sam McGuffin stows away on Santa's sleigh one Christmas
Eve, intending to visit the North Pole, but instead he discovers the
secret island paradise where Santa and his elves vacation every year
when their work is done.
  ISBN 978-0-8037-3126-4
  [1. Stowaways—Fiction. 2. Islands—Fiction. 3. Beaches—Fiction.
4. Santa Claus—Fiction. 5. Christmas—Fiction.] I. Title.
  PZ7.B4822Se 2009
  [E]—dc22
                          2009004156

The illustrations for this book were created using watercolor and acrylic paint, colored pencil, and Photoshop.

Sam McGuffin couldn't resist. When he heard the muffled sound of reindeer hooves, he tugged on his sneakers, climbed out the window, and smuggled himself into the back of Santa's sleigh! What kid wouldn't grab the chance for a magical Christmas Eve ride to the North Pole?

But the North Pole wasn't their destination that night. After Santa and the reindeer finished their rounds in hyper-speed . . .

. . . they landed on the most beautiful beach Sam had ever seen.
He kept himself hidden as the reindeer settled in for ocean-side
spa treatments.

Just as Sam was getting up the nerve to go exploring, an elf discovered him. "Stowaway!" shouted the elf, and all of the others came running. Santa followed, spiffy in his off-duty clothing.

"I'm sorry," said Sam. "I just wanted to see what your workshop looked like. I didn't mean to cause trouble."

Santa chuckled at that, and so Sam dared to say something else. "I sure want to thank you, Santa, for all the great presents every year."

"You know," said Santa, "I've never actually heard a child say that before. I get thousands of letters with requests, but never any thanks." He laughed. "You're welcome, Sam McGuffin. Merry Christmas!"

Then Santa surprised Sam again.
"Would you like to be the first guest ever
to tour our vacation getaway?" he asked.

Sam was overjoyed. And even though everything on the island was elf-sized, he seemed to fit in just fine.

The elves kept the photos to prove it.

After the amusement park, it was time for the beach.
Sam couldn't help laughing at Santa's bathing suit.

He sure didn't laugh at Santa's rad surfing skills, though. Sam had never seen anyone hang ten like that before.

The fun continued. Sam did things
he never dreamed he'd do,

like play soccer with nutcracker soldiers . . .

and dodgeball at 3,000 feet.

Sunset meant it was time for the Wish Dinner. All you
had to do was imagine your favorite food and it instantly
appeared on your plate! Sam thought it was pretty funny
that one of the elves wished for shrimp.

For dessert they all ate candy ornaments from enormous chocolate Christmas trees.

Santa let Sam stay for the talent show, but then it was time to go home. After a long good-bye hug, Sam said, "I wish there was something I could do to thank you, Santa."

"Actually, there is," replied Santa with a chuckle. "Everyone leaves me milk and cookies on Christmas Eve, but I'd much prefer pretzels and ginger ale." Sam promised he wouldn't forget.

It was foggy that night, so Santa asked a certain reindeer to fly his guest home.

When they arrived, it was as if no time had passed. Sam snuck into bed and was soon smiling in his sleep as he dreamed about the remarkable adventure he'd just had.

Christmas morning was as jolly as ever, with the whole family enjoying their gifts and their time together.

And then it got even better! Sam glanced back at the tree and suddenly noticed one more unopened gift. The tag read "For Sam."

Thankfulness is the secret to happiness. —S.C.